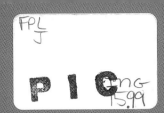

Me dedicate this book to Heather and to Holly and Emily.
Me happy.

Copyright © 2008 by Jeremy Tankard

First edition 2008

Library of Congress Cataloging-in-Publication Data
Tankard, Jeremy.
Me hungry! / Jeremy Tankard. — 1st ed.
p. cm.
Summary: A little prehistoric boy decides to hunt for his own food and makes a new friend in the process.
ISBN 978-0-7636-3360-8
[1. Prehistoric peoples — Fiction. 2. Animals — Fiction.] I. Title.

PZ7.T161613Me 2008
[E] — dc22
2007035735

2 4 6 8 10 9 7 5 3 1

Printed in China

This book was typeset in Stone Hinge.
The illustrations were created using ink and digital media.

Candlewick Press
2067 Massachusetts Avenue
Cambridge, Massachusetts 02140

visit us at www.candlewick.com

ME HUNGRY!

Jeremy Tankard

CANDLEWICK PRESS
CAMBRIDGE, MASSACHUSETTS

Me hungry!

Hey, me hungry!

Me hungry.

Me eat rabbit!

No. Me hide!

Me eat porcupine!

No! Me sharp!

You not sharp.
You not mean.

We friends!